Knitty Kitty

DAVID ELLIOTT

illustrated by CHRISTOPHER DENISE

CANDLEWICK PRESS
CAMBRIDGE, MASSACHUSETTS

First edition 2008. Library of Congress Cataloging-in-Publication Data is available. Library of Congress Catalog Card Number 2007052160. ISBN 978-0-7636-3169-7. This book was typeset in Stempel Schneidler. The illustrations were done in acrylic and ink on paper. Candlewick Press, 2067 Massachusetts Avenue, Cambridge, Massachusetts 02140. Visit us at www.candlewick.com. Printed in China. 10 9 8 7 6 5 4 3 2 1

To Kris Liberman. Andy Hollinger, too—
the coolest cats I know.
D. E.

For my mom
C. D.

Clickety-click.
Tickety-tick.
Knitty Kitty sits and knits.

"A hat for me, Knitty Kitty?"

"Yes, little kitten. A hat. To keep you cozy."

Tickety-tick.
Clickety-click.
Knitty Kitty sits and knits.

"Mittens for me, Knitty Kitty?"

"Yes, little kitten. Mittens.
To keep you toasty."

Clickety-click.
Lickety-split.
Knitty Kitty sits and knits.

"A hat for me, Knitty Kitty?
Mittens for me?"

"No, little kitten. A scarf. To keep you comfy."

But snowmen like to be cozy, too.
At least, that's what kittens think.

The winter moon rises.
Knitty Kitty rings her bell.

It's bedtime for kittens everywhere.

"Come along, little kittens."

But the kittens can't sleep.
"We're not cozy!" they meow. "We're not comfy. We're not toasty!"

"Don't worry," purrs Knitty Kitty.
"I have something to keep you warm."

"What is it, Knitty Kitty?" the kittens cry.

"Night-night, little kittens."

"Night-night, Knitty Kitty."

"Night-night."

"Night-night."

"Night-night."